# GOODNIGHT,
# VEGGIES

# Diana Murray and Zachariah OHora

HOUGHTON MIFFLIN HARCOURT  BOSTON  NEW YORK

Sunset in the garden.

Robins in their nest.

Tossing, turning veggies

need to get some rest.

# Turnips tucked in tightly.

Potatoes closing eyes.

Tuckered-out tomatoes

humming lullabies.

Cuddly cauliflowers.

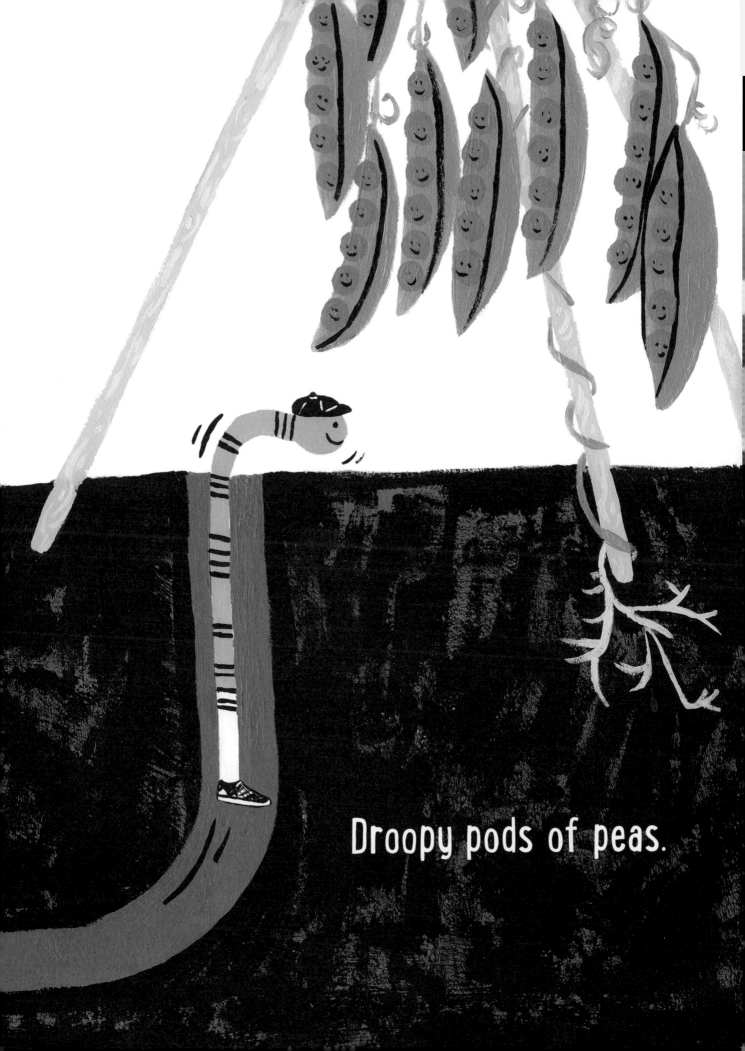

Droopy pods of peas.

Rhubarbs reading stories
to worn-out broccolis.

Baby carrots snuggling.
Baby lettuce too.

Baby eggplants dreaming . . .

of places far and new.

Zzzz

Zzzzz

Zzzz

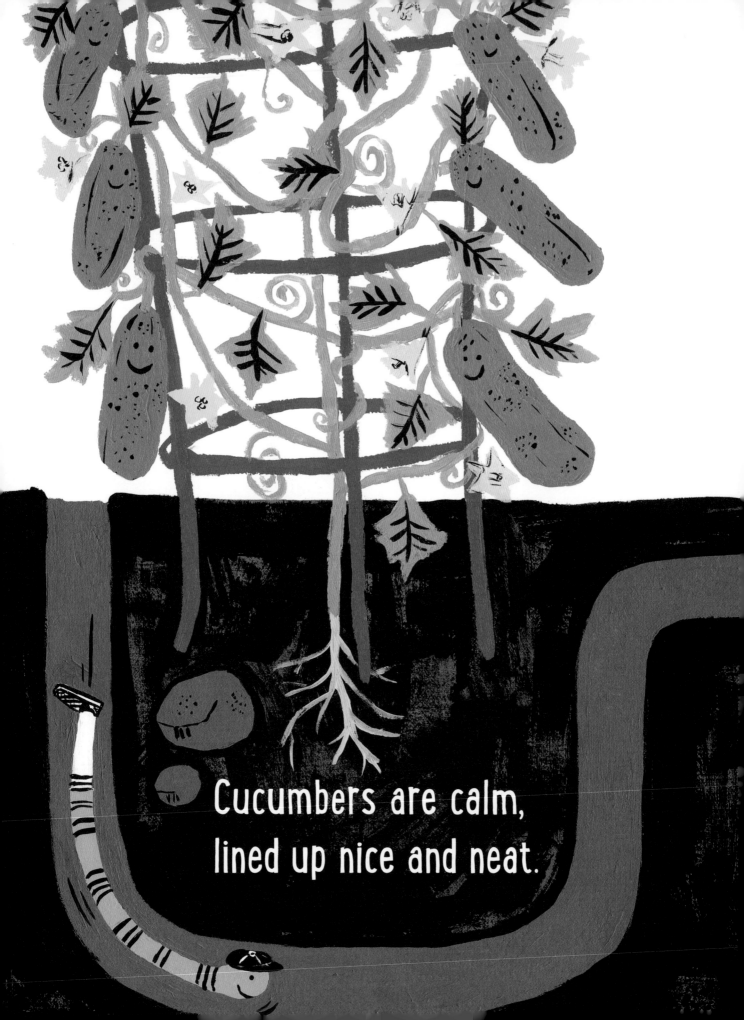

Cucumbers are calm,
lined up nice and neat.

Golden yams are still.

And beets are simply beat.

Cabbages are nodding
their leafy, sleepy heads.

# Radishes are dozing in cozy garden beds.

Celery is snoring
as sunset disappears.

Cranky corn rolls over
and covers up its ears.

Every veggie's snoozing,

beneath the moon so bright,

for nothing's more exhausting

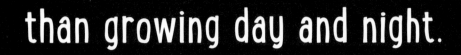
# than growing day and night.

# Goodnight, sleepy veggies!
## Sleep tight!

For my parents, who taught me to love veggies —D.M.

For Lydia, who has never met a veggie she couldn't stick in vinegar —Z.O.

hmhbooks.com

The illustrations in this book were created with 100% vegetarian printmaking paper and acrylic paint.
The text type was set in LunchBox. · The display type was set in YWFT Ultramagnetic Rough. · Book design by Jessica Handelman

Library of Congress Cataloging-in-Publication Data · Names: Murray, Diana, author. | OHora, Zachariah, illustrator.
Title: Goodnight, veggies / written by Diana Murray ; illustrated by Zachariah OHora. · Description: Boston ; New York : Houghton Mifflin
Harcourt, [2020] | Summary: Illustrations and easy-to-read rhyming text invite the reader to
a community garden where potatoes close their eyes, cabbages nod their heads, and corn covers its ears to go to sleep.
Identifiers: LCCN 2019007461 | ISBN 9781328866837 (hardcover picture book)
Subjects: | CYAC: Stories in rhyme. | Bedtime–Fiction. | Vegetables–Fiction. | Community gardens–Fiction. | Gardens–Fiction.
Classification: LCC PZ8.3.M9362 Goo 2020 | DDC [E]–dc23 · LC record available at https://lccn.loc.gov/2019007461

Manufactured in China · SCP 10 9 8 7 6 5 4 3 2 1 · 4500785262